TOBY TUCKER

Hogging all the Pig Swill

Also by Val Wilding

TOBY TUCKER

Hogging all the Pig Swill

VAL WILDING

Illustrated by Michael Broad

EGMONT

For the real Toby Tucker – you know who you are!

EGMONT
We bring stories to life

Published in Great Britain 2007
by Egmont UK Limited
239 Kensington High Street, London W8 6SA

Text copyright © 2007 Val Wilding
Cover and illustrations copyright © 2007 Michael Broad

The moral rights of the author and illustrator have been asserted

ISBN 978 1 4052 2548 9

1 3 5 7 9 10 8 6 4 2

A CIP catalogue record for this title is available
from the British Library

Printed and bound in Great Britain by the CPI Group

The Allen house, present day

Toby Tucker looked round his bedroom with complete and utter satisfaction. Not a fairy in sight!

'Looks good, doesn't it?' said his foster-father, Don.

Toby nodded happily. 'Worth waiting for!'

He'd actually had to wait ages for Don and Evie to work their way through decorating the house before they got to his room at the top. Toby's walls had originally been pink – very pink – and plastered with fairies.

Evie came in with mugs of tea and a plate of home-made plum jam tarts. They weren't as good-looking as shop ones, but they tasted a whole lot better, especially when they were still warm.

Don took the tray and kicked a chair towards Evie. 'Sit down, love,' he said.

Toby munched contentedly. He thought, for

the hundredth time, how lucky he was. Just a few months ago, he'd been living in the children's home, then the first magical thing happened when Don and Evie became his foster parents. Now he had a home, two dogs and a sort-of-family.

Evie got up. 'We'd better bring your things back in from the landing,' she said. 'You'll want your chest tonight, I expect.'

Toby nodded. The wooden chest was the second magical thing that had happened to him – but in this case it literally *was* magic.

Evie went to pull it in, but Don stopped her. 'No, you don't.' She smiled and squeezed his arm.

Once all Toby's clutter was back in, he started to straighten the room. The chest went beneath the window, the books on the shelves, junky stuff under his bed and so on. He couldn't hang his pinboard up, because the hook had gone. He stood it against the wall and examined it as he nibbled the last jam tart.

Five names. Five ancestors. Five magical lives.

'Tob-eeee!' Evie called. 'Can you come?'

'On my way!' Toby galloped downstairs and joined his foster parents at the kitchen table. 'What?'

Don and Evie glanced at each other.

'What?' Toby said again.

'The most amazing thing's happened,' said Don. 'We thought we couldn't – but it seems we can . . . Toby, Evie's going to have a baby.'

'Oh. Oh, that's great,' said Toby. 'Er, when?'

'A few months yet,' said Evie. 'Toby, we really

want you to be pleased.'

'Oh, I am,' said Toby. He looked down at the table. 'Wow.'

Don stood up. 'Come on, lad. I'll knock a hook in for your pinboard.'

Toby made for the door. 'No, it's OK. Tomorrow will do. You two, er, talk.'

He flew upstairs.

+ + +

Toby had trouble sleeping that night. A baby. It would be Don and Evie's very own.

He tossed and rolled and fidgeted. Finally, he sat up and asked himself the question that had nagged him since he'd heard about the baby. 'Will they want me any more?'

By three o'clock in the morning, the question had turned into a statement. 'They won't want me any more.'

He fell into a deep sleep, and woke with a start when Evie brought him a cup of tea. She hung around, and Toby knew she was waiting for him to speak, but he didn't know what to say. She smiled at him and left.

After breakfast, Toby raced back upstairs. 'The new baby will know exactly who he is,' he thought. 'It's even more important now that I find out who *I* am.'

He went to his wooden chest. The children's home people had absolutely no idea who he was or where he came from. The only clue they had was Toby's chest. He opened it. It was full of scraps of torn paper. Buried beneath them was a framed photograph.

Toby took it out and examined the gentle old face. As always, he got a warm feeling as he did so.

'Who are you?' he asked the photo. 'Are you my ancestor?' He turned the photo over and read, for what seemed like the thousandth time, the pencilled note on the back.

'When you come from'. It wasn't a mistake. Gee, whoever he was, did mean 'when' you come from, not 'where'.

> The paper in the chest is your family tree. I wonder which little baby tore it up, eh, Toby Tucker? Piece it together and you'll find out who you are and when you come from.
>
> Gee.

That was the chest's magical secret. Those names on the pinboard were the names of real people – people who'd once lived, and whose lives Toby had, sort of, shared. Each time he'd pieced one of those names together, the magic had begun.

He scooped out a heap of scraps, spread them out on the deep red carpet and picked out a couple of likely looking pieces. One had 'olas' on it. That could be Nicholas. The other had 'Pres'. That was obviously the beginning of a name.

He thought of the baby. Would he have to leave? Suddenly Toby felt a terrible urgency – a desperate need to find out who he was. Frantically, he sorted through the paper scraps.

'Orin . . . Gris . . . mel . . .'

'Looks like you could do with some help!' said a voice from the doorway.

'Jake!' said Toby.

'And me!' said Amber, as Toby's two best friends sauntered in.

'Wow!' Jake admired the room. 'Great colour – like the stripy blind.'

Amber stuck out her bottom lip. 'I liked the fairies,' she said.

The others stared. She burst out laughing and flopped on to the floor. 'Ah, your family tree! We'll help, won't we, Jake?'

That was the last thing Toby wanted, but he felt it would be mean to say so. 'OK,' he said, 'but promise me, if you find two bits that go together, you'll let me actually join them?'

They nodded.

He shrugged. 'It's sort of special for me to do it – it's my family tree.'

'I know,' said Jake. 'It's all you've got.'

Amber poked him. 'It's not, stupid. He's got all his stuff here, and he's got Don and Evie, too, and the dogs.'

Toby didn't say anything.

They'd been shuffling countless bits of paper when Amber's mobile rang. 'Got to go,' she said. 'I'm getting some new shoes!' She dashed off. 'See ya!'

Jake shook his head. 'Fancy getting excited over new shoes.' He leaned over. 'What've you got? "Barrow"? Look, I've got "Fred" – they'd go together, wouldn't they?'

Toby's heart thumped. 'No,' he lied. 'The edges are different.'

Jake flung 'Fred' down and Toby swiftly slipped it into his own hand. 'Let's pack up,' he said.

'No, I'm OK for a bit longer.'

'To-beee!' came Evie's voice. 'Iced lemonade and choc chip cookies in the garden. Come and get some fresh air.'

'I'll go,' said Jake. 'See if she'll let us bring it up here, then we can carry on.' He started downstairs. 'Bet they're home-made cookies – I smelled them on the way in.'

Toby picked up 'Barrow'. He'd put that with 'Fred' later, when he was alone.

His hand tingled. He opened it. 'They're together!' he said. 'I had the pieces together in my hand! It's started!' He quickly laid the two scraps side by side on the carpet and watched.

A drawing began to appear beside the name 'Fred Barrow'. It was a boy in short trousers. Toby waited for it to change – it always had done before – into a drawing of himself.

'There I am,' he breathed, 'and now . . .'

Just as he expected, the drawing morphed back into the boy in short trousers. It began to shimmer. The shimmer grew into a column of silvery

light that moved towards Toby. He held his breath waiting for the feeling of cold jelly slithering down into his tummy. As the silvery column shimmered over him, it happened. 'Brrr-rrr!' Toby shivered.

He stood up and turned, knowing that in the window, instead of the chest, would be . . .

Fred Barrow!

Toby felt pulled towards the boy. His knees hit the bed, so he climbed on to it. The magnetic force was so strong he couldn't stay upright. The room seemed to whirl, making his head spin. He fell forwards, bounced off the bed on to the floor and rolled into the boy.

He wasn't hurt. He just felt so sleepy. And not very well. Not well at all.

Aug 31st 1939, just before the war

Sisters! I was having a nice cosy doze this morning, when Rose bellowed at me, 'Fred Barrow, stop bouncing on that bed! You'll have the ceiling down in Mrs Little's flat!'

Little Mrs Little's place is that much of a tip, she'd never notice if a few chunks of ceiling plaster came down. Anyway, bouncing on the bed? Me? I'm ill! How could I bounce on the bed? Mind, it was a bit strange, because as I opened my eyes, I remember thinking the room was moving. But maybe the room was still and the bed was moving. I certainly felt as if something had just landed on me.

I told Mum, and she said measles makes you feel a bit odd sometimes. 'I'm off to the shops now, love,' she said. 'Rose is going to meet Lynn, and Berry's coming to sit with you.'

Aargh! Isn't having measles bad enough, without being entertained by Berry Little? I'd sooner have Eric to keep me company – dogs just lie there and let you do what you want, but Mum won't let him in the bedroom.

Berry's always around. She likes being up in our flat because it's tidy, she says. Her mum's a real scruff. Berry fusses over me because when I was a baby, she dropped me – on my head. She's felt guilty ever since, Dad says, but I don't think she should. I reckon that's what made me so brainy.

Berry thinks I'm still about four, I reckon. She brings things for me to do, now I'm getting better. Yesterday she had me tracing pictures with paper from the lavvy. Today she brought in a tin tray and a huge lump of plasticine.

'We're going to make a zoo today, Freddy,' she said. 'Let's plump your pillows and get started.'

I made a lion with three legs, and a two-tailed monkey, but you can't annoy Berry. When she made a pond out of a big tin lid full of water, I put half a penguin in with the crocodile, as if it had been eaten. She didn't care! 'Freddy, you are a one!' she said.

'D'you think I'll be going back to school soon?' I asked her. Not that I want to.

'There might not be a school to go to,' she said, 'not if the war starts. Here, have some more plasticine. You can make an elephant.'

War talk gives me the shivers. Mum and Dad have talked about nothing else but whether or not we're going to war against Germany. Dad's spending more and more time at his office. He works in a big government building in the middle of London.

I thought of my new *Beano* comic under the bed. If I leaned over I could just see Big Eggo's beak. There was a story in there I was halfway through. How could she think I'd rather make an elephant than read that? I rolled the plasticine into a heavy ball and dropped it on the tin tray. The three-legged lion keeled over and Berry got a lap full of monkeys.

'Call that an elephant?' she said.

'No,' I said. 'I call it a bomb. Zoo's gone. Can I read now?'

She patted my head and sat quietly beside

me. That's just how I like her.

⤙ ⤙ ⤙

Berry was right. I haven't got a school to go to. At least, I have, but there won't be anyone there. All the children have been evacuated. War has begun!

It's all Germany's fault. Two days ago, they invaded Poland. Next thing, the schools took all the children (if their parents wanted them to go) to the country, to stay with strangers. I can't go because of the measles.

It's weird at night. If you open the curtains, it's all dark, right here in London! No one's allowed to show a light, and if anybody in the street strikes a match for a cigarette at night, they're for it! That's in case bombers come over. If a German pilot saw lots of street lights and house lights, he'd think, 'Hah! This is a good place to drop my bomb.' Then, BOOM!

This morning the Prime Minister, Mr Chamberlain, said on the wireless, 'I have to tell you that this country is now at war with Germany.'

A few minutes after, the air-raid siren went. That was really scary. I'm glad it was Sunday and all our family were at home.

Later

The air-raid siren was a false alarm. Some French plane went over Croydon airport, and they thought it must be German.

Berry said everyone's talking about doing their bit to help the war. That's a good idea. Then it can be over quickly.

I wonder if my mates have been evacuated. I haven't seen them for weeks. Clifford's mum sent a message saying she was sorry I was ill, but she didn't want him to catch measles. She sent a tin of toffees, too. I had no one to share them with, except Berry, and she watches her figure, whatever that means. So I ate the lot. Didn't give Rose any, because she hardly ever comes near me. Too busy talking about film stars with her mate, Skinny Lynnie, I suppose.

It's great to be allowed out, but it's really weird not having my mates around. I took Eric, and my flipping gas mask, and went to ask if Jeffrey and John could come out to play, but their mum went all teary-eyed and said they've been evacuated.

I went to find Colin. He's gone as well. His nan asked why I was still around, so I said I'd had measles.

'I expect your

parents will make other arrangements for you,' she said.

'I don't think so,' I said, and she raised her eyebrows at me – one of them's got a long straggly hair. Every time I see it I want to yank it out.

Then I went round to Uncle Jim's shop. He's a butcher, and he's usually got something nice to eat under the counter. Not meat, I don't mean – he swaps sausages and things for cakes or buns from the baker next door.

'Hello, son!' he said. Obviously I'm not his son, but that's what he calls me. He even calls his errand boy 'son'.

'All better?' he asked. 'You'll be getting evacuated any day, won't you?'

He tossed a chunk of sausage meat to Eric.

I took a sticky bun from the bag he gave me. 'No, I missed evacuation. I'm not going. I'm staying here to do my bit.'

He smiled. 'And what does my sister say about that?'

His sister's my mum. 'She doesn't say anything,' I said. 'She's too busy trying to get Rose to help her with the housework.'

Uncle Jim laughed. 'That girl! Head full of fluff, I reckon!'

I laughed.

'Want a job?' Uncle Jim asked.

I nodded.

'Take this to the crabby woman at 4 Lime Lane,' he said. 'You'll get a tanner when you get back.'

Sixpence! Enough for a Dandy and some sweets! Apart from not having my mates around, and getting glared at by the crabby woman, me and Eric had a good day today.

I went home and got changed for Cubs. Rose

laughed when she saw me. 'Waste of time that is,' she said. 'There's no Cubs any more.'

I didn't believe her, but Mum said, 'Sorry, love, I forgot to tell you. Cubs has been disbanded. Akela's gone and joined up in something – don't know what, but she's gone to do her bit, anyway.'

Rotten. That's rotten. I liked Cubs.

I go to Uncle Jim's every weekday, to run errands. Instead of money, he gives me meat for Mum. She says it saves a lot and makes the housekeeping go much further. That's good, but I wish she'd give me more pocket money.

Today, I'd just got back to Uncle Jim's shop after a delivery, when he said, 'Want to come for a ride, son?'

I got in the van, with Eric on my lap, nearly suffocating me.

'I want to fill up with petrol,' said Uncle Jim. 'Heard a rumour that it might be rationed soon.'

Good. If he can't drive the van, I can do more

deliveries for him. Maybe I'll get money as well as meat.

We got in a traffic jam. Uncle Jim switched the engine off to save petrol, and when he tried to restart, it coughed and spluttered. He got the starting handle and went round the front to get it going. 'What's the hold-up?' he called to a cyclist coming the other way.

'Petrol queue,' she said. 'Panic buying! Stupid fools.'

Uncle Jim nodded. 'Stupid,' he agreed. Then he winked at me.

He says quite a few things might be in short

supply. The government will ration them if they are, so everybody gets a fair share.

I'd better tell Mum and Dad.

Later

I told them. They tried hard not to laugh.

'Thank you for telling us,' they said. 'That's very helpful.'

Rose said afterwards that everybody knows rationing might happen. 'Don't you think Father knows about this sort of thing?' she said. 'He does work for the government, you know.'

If they're going to ration things, she'd better stock up with shampoo and soap and face cream. She washes her hair *every* Friday night!

Our Anderson shelter's arrived. Me and Dad helped the men unload our one. It was delivered in corrugated steel sheets. Uncle Jim came and helped us dig a pit, three feet deep, in the garden.

The Littles share the garden with us.

Even though we're all sharing the shelter, Mrs Little didn't help us. Uncle Jim said he wouldn't expect her to dig, because she's so tiny, but she could have brought us a cuppa. Dad said, 'I wouldn't drink out of her cups if you paid me.'

We bolted the steel sheets together. When the shelter was in place, we piled earth on top, really deep. If there's an air raid, we'll have to go down to the shelter until it's over. Mum's promised to make it comfortable. Suppose we have to sleep in there? I'd have Berry fussing over me all night!

Rose came back from Skinny Lynnie's house with very curly hair. I laughed, and she said, 'You're so stupid. This is the very latest look.'

Dad said, 'Been busy, Rose?' and she said yes. She's so dense, she didn't realise he was being sarcastic. When she saw the shelter, she said, 'You won't catch me dead in that thing.' Dad shook his head and rolled his eyes, so I did, too, but she saw me and clipped me round the ear.

I cheered up when she realised she'd forgotten her gas mask, and had to go back for it. I stuck my tongue out at her and went with Dad to listen to *ITMA* on the wireless. It was really funny. Makes a change from all the serious stuff. There's too much news and talk these days.

✈ ✈ ✈

I can't believe it! I'm being evacuated! On my own! All my mates went off together, so they wouldn't have been as scared as me.

Mum says they were scared. They were put on a train, with labels tied to them, she said, and their parents weren't allowed on the platform because it was too crowded. She says I'll be fine because she'll take me, and I'm going to stay with friends.

'I don't know them!' I said. 'How can they be friends?'

'Dot and I went to school together,' said Mum.

Just because they were friends doesn't mean I'll like them. Mum says Dot married a farmer called Ken, and they've got every sort of animal. I'll love it there, she says.

I wonder if they've got guinea pigs. I've always wanted a guinea pig.

✦ ✦ ✦

The train was crowded and hot. A lot of the men were in uniform, and some ladies, too. I wondered if they were going off to war, but I don't suppose you'd go by train. By the time we unpacked our egg sandwiches, they were so warm they stunk the carriage out. I wasn't hungry, so I didn't eat much. A soldier next to Mum polished off what we didn't want. Everyone was glad when they'd gone.

It was dark when we reached the farm, and they had dinner waiting for us. It was steak and kidney pie, with mashed spuds and cabbage, and as much gravy as you wanted. I was starving. Mum stayed the night and got up early to go back to London. I begged her not to leave me, but she said she must look after Dad and Rose, and I'll be fine.

'I won't.'

Then she said we all have to make sacrifices because of the war, and we all have to do our bit.

'I don't see how me living alone miles away from home will bother Mr Hitler much,' I said.

She laughed! 'You're not alone. You've got

Auntie Dot and Uncle Ken, and all the animals.'

I'd forgotten about the animals.

I walked to the end of the drive with Mum. I didn't cry. Well, not so she saw. When I went back to the farmhouse, Auntie Dot was at the door. She put an arm round me and said, 'Like to help me feed the chickens?'

She's nice.

Uncle Ken came in for breakfast at half past nine. I'd already had mine, with Mum, but Auntie Dot didn't mind me having another lot. Uncle Ken said he'd done the cows. I asked what he did to them, and he told me about milking. I never realised all that went on.

It's very green here. There's loads of fields with stuff growing in them. Uncle Ken says he'll be using every square inch of land to grow crops

and vegetables, to help the war effort.

They haven't got any guinea pigs.

Auntie Dot asked me about London. She's been twice, she said, a long time ago. I told her it hadn't changed much since the war started, and she said, 'I expect you have to watch out for spies in London.'

'How can you tell if someone's a spy?' I asked.

'Ooh, I don't know, dear,' she said. 'If they speak with a German accent, I suppose, or if they look a bit odd, or if they're poking their noses into people's secrets, perhaps.'

If that's true, then apart from the German accent, Mrs Little could be a spy!

✈ ✈ ✈

This morning, when I came back from helping Uncle Ken with the pigs, Auntie Dot asked me to collect the eggs while she dished up breakfast. When I fetched the basket I found three letters in it! All for me! She'd put them there to surprise me!

I whizzed round the chicken houses so fast there were feathers all over the place.

Auntie Dot said, 'Read your letters while you eat. You must be fair bursting for news from home.'

I was. Actually, there wasn't much proper news, mainly questions about me. Uncle Jim sent a message in Dad's letter saying he was right, petrol's being rationed. Dad told me bits of war news. I hear a lot of that on the wireless here anyway. Mum said Dad's really tired, because he's been working too hard, and gets grumpy sometimes. She's knitting me a warm pullover. Rose's letter was just about some film she saw. She never told me its name, just went on about what a heartthrob the star was. Really interesting, I don't think. She said Dad's grumpy because the price of beer and fags has gone up.

🐦 🐦 🐦

A woman called Georgina's come to stay here. At least, she looks like a woman to me, but Uncle Ken says she's 'a slip of a lass'. He doesn't think she's strong enough for farm work, but that's what she's here to do. She joined the Women's Land Army. It's not really an army, although Georgina says she'd soon give what-for to any Jerry who parachuted near her. (Jerry is what she calls the Germans.) She says all her friends joined, too, and they're called land girls. They'll do all the tractor-driving and digging and growing things, so young men who work on farms can go off to fight the war.

'Your Uncle Ken's two labourers have gone to do their bit for King and country,' she said. 'Jolly good show, too!'

She's ever so posh. I asked her if she minds working with pigs.

'In these troubled times, Fred,' she said, 'some fly fighter planes, some sail destroyers, and some fight with guns. Daddy says if I can do my bit with a spade and a willing heart, then I'll help England win the war.'

Crikey! I only wondered if she minds shovelling pig poo.

+ + +

I'd give anything for a cuddle with my mum, but I do like it here. There's loads to eat. The farm's huge, but Uncle Ken says it's small compared to some. It takes a long time to walk right round it, but you can find things to eat as you go. There's blackberries on the hedge, but Auntie Dot says she wouldn't touch them with a pitchfork, because they're too old. There's apples left on trees, and you can pick them if you want! There's nuts growing, but I haven't got to grips with them. They're either not proper nuts yet, or they're old and bad, and I never seem to get them just right. Besides, when I stamp on them to break them open, I smash them and you can't tell what's shell, what's nut, or what's dirt.

✈ ✈ ✈

I've started school. Today only one car went past me on the way there, but I saw lots of horses and carts. They don't need petrol!

The school's ever so small. Usually, there's only one teacher, and about fourteen children. I couldn't believe that at first. There's thirty-six in my old class.

There are other evacuated kids here. Most come from one school in East London. They've brought two teachers with them, so there's three classes. The trouble is you can hear all the lessons at once. Wish we could learn three lots of stuff in one go!

Today we had air-raid practice. We walked silently, no running, across the playground to the shelter. We had our gas masks, and some cotton

wool to put in our ears so we didn't go deaf when the bombs went off. Everyone was really sensible. In my old class, someone would have mucked about behind the teachers' backs. We also had our clothes checked to make sure they had our names in. A boy told me that's so they can identify the dead bodies. Gives me the shivers, that does.

It was misty this morning. When it's foggy at home, it's a nuisance, but here it's more see-through. Bit scary when you're walking along a quiet lane and a horse's head suddenly appears out of the mist. I know how to feed horses without getting bitten now. Nobody ever showed me that before.

I had a letter from Berry today. I felt a bit miserable after I read it. I know I go on about her, but she's a bit like a sister, only one that likes you. Rose hasn't written since that first letter. And I did write back to her. At least, I think I did. Can't remember for sure.

Dinner tonight was ham, two eggs and a mountain of fried potatoes. For afters, we had hot treacle pudding with custard. Me, Georgina and Uncle Ken had seconds. Ooh, it was lovely!

34

A letter from Mum! She says Dad's really busy, and sometimes sleeps on a camp bed in the office. Uncle Jim crashed his car in the blackout and broke his nose. It must be dangerous with no traffic lights and no car lights. Rose complains all the time, Mum says, because there's never any dance music on the wireless when she wants it, and the cinema's closed. Hard cheddar, that's what I think.

The weather's been quite warm up till now, but I'm not sure living on a farm's going to be so nice in the winter. I hope the war finishes before it gets really cold.

I've learned how to make pig swill. That's their food. It's easy – you moosh all the potato peelings and cabbage stumps and apple cores together, and you can put in scrapings from your plates, too – not that I've ever got much left on mine. The important thing is never to put coffee grounds in pig swill (we don't have coffee because Auntie Dot thinks it poisons your liver), or rhubarb leaves. Well, I've never seen a rhubarb outside a pie, so I wouldn't recognise a leaf if I saw one. And we never put meat in it, because our pigs are vegetarians.

The pigs love swill. They stick their heads right in it, and snort and snuffle! They're funny. I know they smell, but you don't notice after you've been round them a bit. It hits you when you first go near the sties, though.

I found a kid – one of the London vaccies – in tears on the way to school today. It was pouring, so he'd taken a short cut across a field and didn't see that the gate to the next field was open. He heard a noise and looked round to see a herd of cows running after him. The poor thing tripped and found himself lying in mud with cows all round him and he couldn't see the way out.

He was filthy and half sobbing and half sniffing. 'I ain't never seen a cow till I come 'ere,' he said, 'only in a book. I fort they'd be like the size of dogs.'

'And I thought pigs smelled like violets,' I said. That made him laugh. His name's Orris. My mate Clifford always used to make me laugh. I wish I was at home. Bet that kid does, too.

It always rains on Saturday when there's no school! Me and Uncle Ken still had to do the cows and pigs – Georgina's gone to visit her mum and dad for the day. At least, I think that's what she meant. She went on about 'the jolly old homestead' and 'pater and mater'. Funny woman.

Mr Churchill said on the wireless that eight Nazi planes have been shot down. He's the First

Lord of the Admiralty or something – Dad's met him, and says he knows his stuff.

Whenever I see one of our own planes, I think how terrible it would be to be inside it when it was shot down. I know the pilots have parachutes, but suppose the bullets went through the parachute and made a hole in it – would it still work?

→ → →

Orris sticks to me at school. He's staying with a woman called Miss White. She hasn't got children, so she doesn't really know about boys. Orris says he just bumbles along and as long as he doesn't bother her or her cat, she doesn't bother him.

'When I got 'ere,' he said, 'she give me a barf. I ain't never been in a barf before. It were lovely, all warm. You should've seen me feet when I got out! All clean and white, they was.'

From what I hear, half the evacuees brought more than their gas mask with them. Lots brought nits and fleas as well. Orris said he had loads. 'Miss White didn't 'ave fleas in 'er house when I came,' he said. 'Not even on the cat!'

I got a parcel when I got back to the farm, with the pullover Mum knitted. I don't really like it, so I'll keep it for best. Tomorrow I'm helping Georgina clean out the pigs' trough. The first time I did that, one of the little piglets nipped my leg. I danced round the sty, slipped in a heap of you-know-what and ended up on my back, legs in the air, shouting for my mum!

And pigs are supposed to be vegetarians! Perhaps I should tie a label to my leg, saying, 'Meat. Don't Eat.' Hey! That's a poem!

Orris came to tea today. He's a bit of a pig at the table. He grabs food instead of saying, 'Please pass the whatever,' which is what Auntie Dot likes. She didn't say anything, though. I think she thinks he's all right.

Afterwards, I showed Orris the farm. He liked the pigs. I think that's because they're in sties, nice and safe. I showed him how to scratch them. They love that. I like the rough feel of their skin.

I said, 'Horrible being away from home, isn't it?'

'I do miss me mates,' said Orris. 'I ain't allowed to play in the street 'ere. If a kid comes round and asks me to go down the river or find conkers, Miss White says we 'ave to play in the garden. So nobody comes much.'

'Is your dad a soldier?'

'Ain't got a dad,' Orris said. 'Got a nuncle. When I grow up, I'll be a soldier wiv a gun, and I'll fight that 'itler.'

I said it would have to be a very long war if

he was going to have a chance to fight in it. 'We can't join the forces for years,' I said, 'but we can do our bit in other ways.'

'How?'

'I don't know,' I said. 'But I'll think of something. I always do.'

When I got back to the farm, there was a letter from Berry, with a postal order in it, so I can buy some sweets down at the village shop. Orris can share. He doesn't have much, only what Miss White spares him. Her idea of sweets is a bag of peppermints shaped like headache tablets. Orris says they're so strong they nearly blow your socks off.

I'm going home! Mum's letter says she's coming for me on Thursday! She says the war doesn't seem to be coming to much, and people reckon it's safe for kids to go home.

I can't wait!

41

Tomorrow I leave the farm. After school, I went
round saying goodbye to people. Some of them
asked for my address, and said they'll write.

Orris cried when I said goodbye. Miss White
stood behind him, but as I turned away, she took
hold of his hand, very gently.

He'll be OK. I hope.

I was up before the cows this morning, all packed
and ready. I was dressed too smart for milking,
but I went and watched anyway. Afterwards I

said goodbye to the chickens and ducks. Then it was the pigs and Georgina. I was sorry to say goodbye to all of them.

The pigs are right characters. Uncle Ken doesn't give them names – he says it's not worth it. I think it is, so my leaving present to the three big ones was names. They're called Goofy, Mickey and Donald. Georgina promised to call them that.

When I said goodbye to her, she swooped down and hugged me. Then she came out with one of her mouthfuls. 'Chin up, old bean,' she said. 'The war won't last for ever. England has a great machine behind her. We're all doing our bit, and if we all pull together to help the chaps, we'll beat Jerry at his own game.'

I'm not doing my bit, am I? I know I've helped on the farm, and Uncle Ken says it's the farmers who feed Britain, but what can I do at home? Maybe I can grow carrots and cabbages in the garden. No, not cabbages. We'd be eating them every day. I couldn't stand that. Wish you could grow chocolate!

It was lovely when Mum came, but I sort of expected we'd go straight off to the station. Auntie Dot wasn't having that! We had a huge lunch, then she packed up ham sandwiches, apples, a flask of tea for Mum, and a bottle of milk for me. Mum couldn't believe the milk was in the cow just a few hours ago!

The train was full of soldiers, sailors and airmen, drinking bottles of beer and laughing.

People tried to read, but it was too dingy. There was only a little blue light in the carriage. I leaned against my mum.

It was dark and foggy when we reached London. Pitch-dark. We queued for the bus, and it was funny standing waiting, and seeing nothing because the shops and houses had no lights. You'd have thought the world was asleep, except for voices and clattering footsteps, and cars creeping past. When the bus came, a man at the front of the queue got a tiny torch out. He shone it on his feet, then quickly flashed it on and off, so the driver would see us. When we sat down, Mum said, 'It is eerie, isn't it, being so dark? You'll get used to it.'

It was worse when we got off. We had to walk along two roads, and the fog had got thicker. Mum gave me a newspaper to hold in front of me. 'You need something light,' she said, 'so people can see you in time to swerve out of the way.'

When we reached home, Mum couldn't get

the key out because her arms were full, so she knocked – three knocks, so Mrs Little would know it wasn't for her. The door flew open and there was Rose.

'Put that light out!' shouted a man's voice from inside the fog.

Rose quickly slammed the door. I think she swore, too. A moment later, she opened it again. She'd put the hall light out. 'That air-raid warden's always shouting at me,' she complained. 'Hello, Fred. Welcome home. It's been quiet without you.' And she ruffled my hair!

When we got upstairs, Mum went mad because Dad was due home any minute, and Rose hadn't even started getting his dinner ready. But

Berry galloped up to welcome me home and she set to and peeled the potatoes.

I couldn't speak when I saw Dad. He hugged me and said I'd grown about a foot. 'I'm glad you're home, Fred,' he said. 'It wouldn't be a proper Christmas without you.'

That shook me. I never thought they'd leave me with someone else at Christmas.

Berry wanted to hear all my news. I told her about the milking, and collecting the eggs, and all about the pigs.

'I'm just dishing up, young man,' said Mum. 'I'd rather we didn't have pigs with our dinner.'

Good job they never met Orris.

When I woke this morning, I looked out expecting everything to be different. But it wasn't, not really. The only thing I could see, if I leaned right out, was the ARP place down on the corner, where the air-raid warden has his post. It's got sandbags all round it, so it won't get hit by flying glass or

metal or bricks if a bomb lands nearby. Perhaps we should all have sandbags round our houses! Or we could tie sand-bags to our bodies! That wouldn't be any good for Rose. Dad says she's incapable of lifting anything heavier than a knife and fork. If she doesn't pull her finger out and help Mum more, he says, she'll have to get a job.

This is a funny war. I expected to see planes flying over all the time, shooting at each other. But nothing seems to be happening. Dad says there's plenty to come, and we shouldn't wish it to happen. I wasn't wishing. I was just wondering, that's all.

First thing this morning, Clifford's mum came round. I thought perhaps Clifford was back, but she burst into tears and said that his sister's gone away to be a land girl.

Mum was kind to her for a bit, but then she got fed up with all the dripping and said, 'She's just like lots of other young people – she wants to do her bit.'

Our Rose'll never do her bit. Not if she can help it.

But I want to do my bit. The last war was four years long, and even if this one lasted five years, I wouldn't be old enough to join the forces. I must find another way to do my bit.

One good thing came out of Clifford's mum coming round. She suddenly said, 'You've got your Fred back.'

Obviously.

'Then I don't care what my hubby says,' she went on, 'I'm sending for my Clifford. Jeffrey and John are back, and now Fred is, too, I don't see he can argue with me.'

Jeffrey and John are home and no one told

me! I asked if
I could go out,
and nipped
round to their
house. It was
sunny and didn't feel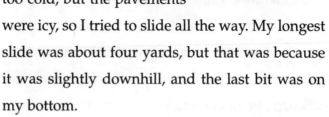
too cold, but the pavements
were icy, so I tried to slide all the way. My longest
slide was about four yards, but that was because
it was slightly downhill, and the last bit was on
my bottom.

Jeffrey and John were in the shed, messing
about with an old pram and a wooden tea chest.
We nattered for a bit, then I asked what they were
doing.

'Cubs,' they said.

'You'd better keep up with the news,' I
jeered. 'Didn't you know Cubs is finished?'

John twanged my braces. 'Didn't you know
that Akela's sister's taken over?'

'It's not proper Cubs,' said Jeffrey. 'But she's

got us together so we can do something to help the war effort.'

'What d'you mean?' I asked.

'We've got to collect waste paper,' said Jeffrey.

'What for?'

'The Prime Minister said paper's going to be in short supply,' he said, 'so if we collect all the paper people have finished with, they take it and make it into important war things, like cartridge wadding, whatever that is.'

'It's for guns,' said John. 'They use paper for making things for aeroplanes, and they can turn it into new paper as well. Don't ask me how.'

This sounded like something useful to do.

Jeffrey suddenly flung down a piece of wood and said, 'I can't do it!'

'Do what?' I said.

'We're trying to turn this box into a collecting cart, but I don't know how to stick the pram wheels on.'

'If I help,' I said, 'can I share the cart?'

'OK.'

I set the two of them to getting the wheels off the pram, while I made a base for the box. Putting the wheels on was a bit sticky, but the coalman came along, and he helped us.

Off we went! We knocked at all the doors in their street. People gave us newspapers, magazines, brown wrapping paper, old letters and all sorts of stuff. Then we took it to Cubs HQ and sorted it into piles. It was all bunged into sacks, ready for someone to collect it.

I decided to do our neighbours on the way home. Mum nearly went mad when I got up to our flat with my arms full of old paper. 'What's all that doing here?'

'I'm taking it to Cubs tomorrow.'

'Oh, I see,' she said. 'It's salvage. Good boy.'

Salvage. I looked it up in Dad's dictionary. One meaning was about saving ships. That wasn't it. Then I found, 'saving and collection of waste material, esp. paper'.

I'm going to do salvage again tomorrow.

Rose is happy! Our local cinema's opened again. She loves going to the flicks. I do, sometimes, but most films are boring, all love stuff. She went to see *Captain Fury* this afternoon. That sounds the sort of thing I'd like, but she wouldn't take me, oh no.

Toad in the hole for dinner. My favourite, and I had loads, because Dad's sleeping at the office tonight.

Well, that was a funny Christmas. For a start, Dad was at work all day, so we had to keep dinner warm till quarter to five. We didn't have a turkey – we had goose instead. It was a present to us all from Auntie Dot and Uncle Ken. I was starving, and we were just about to tuck in when Dad said something about how nice it was for them to rear their own food. I suddenly realised this was one of the geese I used to feed, and refused to eat a mouthful of it. Mum got cross and talked about how if I was so keen on salvaging, how come I was prepared to waste good meat. I said, 'It won't be wasted – Dad'll eat it.' If it hadn't been Christmas Day I'd have got a thick ear for talking back. As it was, I had to eat an awful lot of cabbage.

Everyone (except me) was too full after dinner to do anything much, but we sang some carols and then Berry and Mrs Little came up for a glass of sherry. I had a jigsaw and a huge tin of toffees with a puppy on the front from Berry, and I ate

most of them in bed.

→ → →

I hate it when it's just cold with no snow. I stayed
by the fire today. I got out the new Bayko building
set Dad gave me for Christmas. Mum hates me
playing with it. You stick metal rods in the base,
and you slot the bricks on to them, but sometimes
the rods get stuck. When you manage to tug them
free, you nearly poke your eyes out.

Gracie Fields was on the radio after dinner.
When she sang a song called 'Sally', her voice
went so high it made my hair prickle, and Eric

slunk out on to the landing. Afterwards, Rose tried to sing it. She sounded like a cat when you've accidentally trodden on its tail.

Mum says my flipping school's opening again soon.

Back to school. It's different, because some of the kids are still evacuated, but there's loads of new ones. Ours is the only school open in this area, so some kids have to come by bus.

They don't ring the school bell any more, because a bell's a signal of a poison gas attack, and Miss Elwood doesn't want all the local people

shoving masks on and rushing for the shelters.

The school shelters are big, with benches to sit on. When we have practice, our teacher sometimes makes us put our gas masks on. They're sweaty and the smell's disgusting – it makes me feel sick. And it hurts when you put it on, because it pulls your hair. The girls moan like anything.

A boy called Bill got his gas mask to make a fart noise. He got his legs slapped for that.

Miss Elwood caught me going through the rubbish bin this afternoon. She put her hands on her hips and asked what I thought I was doing. I said, 'Salvaging, Miss,' and she seemed quite pleased.

When I got home today, Rose passed me as I was going indoors.

'Who are you looking at?' she snapped.

'No one,' I said. What was up with her this time?

'I saw you,' she said. 'Don't you dare look at me like that again, or it'll be the worse for you.' And she clipped me round the ear.

'I'm telling Mum,' I said, and ran upstairs, yelling, 'Mu-um! Rose hit me!'

Berry Little ran up after me, and in two seconds flat I'd got her and Mum fussing over me. I'd been pressing my ear hard with my hand, so it was nicely red.

'Rose is cross,' said Mum. 'I went to see Uncle Jim and Auntie Joan, and while I was gone, Rose used a whole week's ration of bacon in sandwiches for her and Lynn.'

Huh! Lynnie won't be so skinny after eating my breakfast!

'I told her she's staying in tonight,' said Mum.

'She's upset because she was going to a dance at the factory where Lynn's dad's the manager. Oh, perhaps I should let her go . . .'

'No!' I said. 'She hit me!'

'Yes, but I feel bad,' said Mum. 'I had a lovely bit of cold beef round at Jim's. Here,' she said, 'I brought a few slices home.' She unwrapped a small greaseproof paper package.

Me, Mum and Berry sat and picked at the cold roast beef, and Rose didn't get any. I kept the greaseproof paper for salvage, but I let Eric lick it first.

⁂

I'm never taking Eric salvaging again. The dentist's receptionist gave me a pile of old magazines. When she'd shut the door, I put them on the pavement, so I could look through for comics to read before I handed them over. A kid from school cycled past and shouted something rude. I couldn't exactly hear what he said, but he always is rude. I stood up to shout back and when I looked down,

Eric had cocked his leg and
peed on the magazines!

I couldn't leave
them there, so I had to
carry them back to Cubs, all
wet and warm and stinking.

→ → →

I had a very late Christmas present today – my
own salvage cart! Dad had it made for me by a
man who works for him, and I had to wait until
they could get it delivered. Can't imagine Dad
bringing that home on the tram! It's heaps better
than Jeffrey and John's! When I was ready to go
salvaging today, Eric jumped in the cart. I know I
said I wasn't going to take him again, but I
thought people might think he's cute, and give
me more stuff. So I let him ride until I'd filled up,
which took practically all afternoon.

I reckon I've got every scrap of paper from all
the streets around. There's not so much about
these days, because I've collected so regularly.

→ → →

There was an air-raid alarm – a real one – at school today. We were in the shelter a long time. Miss Elwood read to us, and another teacher brought a box of wool and knitting needles. I thought she'd make us all knit, but it was only the girls. They let us boys draw. I drew Hitler being chased by a horned bull. I made him really scared.

There are posters everywhere saying 'Dig For Victory'. It means if you've got a garden, grow veg in it. Mum's going to have a go, but I don't think she'll be much good at it. Dad bought her a potted geranium once, and it was dead in a week. When I grew cress on a piece of flannel, she put a saucepan down on it. Crushed cress.

I climbed on the garden wall today to see if the neighbours are digging for victory. They usually have flowers everywhere, even on top of their Anderson shelter. Dad caught me snooping and slapped me. He says it's wrong to spy on people.

🛩 🛩 🛩

By eleven o'clock today I'd only got seven newspapers and a paper bag, so I went home to dig for victory. Mum's bought some seeds, and I read what it said on the packet and planted them properly. Mum watered them. Bet they die now.

I've seen a poster asking for rags to give the troops more blankets. I don't know how they turn rags into blankets, but that's not my problem. I'm off on my rounds again.

🛩 🛩 🛩

Someone called me a champion salvager! I don't go round with the others any more. They're too slow. I go alone. The Lone Salvager, that's me. Today an elderly woman gave me some wool. She said her hands are too stiff to knit any more. I offered to make the poor thing a cup of tea, but she glanced at my hands and said, 'No, thank you. But it's kind of you to offer.'

This is how I can do my bit! I'll be the Lone Salvager (champion), and I'll help people as I go on my rounds.

↝ ↝ ↝

My seeds have turned into little plants. The carrot tops are like some seaweed I saw in Devon – all feathery it was, floating in the water.

There's stuff coming up all over the place! I don't recognise much, but there are definitely carrots. A poster said carrots help you see in the blackout. That would be useful, so I'm going to eat lots.

We've got electricity

in our shelter now, and Mum's made it quite nice, with a bucket to pee in and a place for two of us to sleep at a time. The others have to listen to them snore, Dad says! There's tinned food down there, and a tin opener, and books so we won't get bored. Rose hates the shelter. She's worried her curls will drop out if she's in there for more than five minutes, because of the damp. When it rains, the floor gets wet.

'Better than getting your head blown off,' I said.

Smelling the wet earth reminded me of Auntie Dot's. When I opened the farmhouse door after a rainy night, it smelled like that.

I'm glad to be home, but I miss the animals – the chickens chasing me when I fed them, and the cows following me back to the yard. I liked helping Georgina with the pigs, too. I wonder if she still calls them by their names.

Just as I was thinking about Auntie Dot's I got a letter from Orris!

> Deer Fred I wish you wos back.
> I ate it at Miss Wits, Me mum
> wont let me go back to lUndon
> cos sUmmwUn elsis sleepin in my
> bed. I fink its er sister. Can
> yoU rite to me.
>
> > From Horace

I didn't know that's how you spell his name. He'll always be Orris to me. I wrote back and sent him some comics from my salvage.

— — —

I've been thinking about Orris. Last night I wrote to Auntie Dot and Uncle Ken and said how unhappy he is. I asked if they could get Orris from Miss White and let him live with them. Once he got used to the animals, he'd be happy there. I told them he had fleas at first, but not any more. I hope they think about it.

I wrote my letter while Dad was listening to

Bandwagon. Mum was knitting socks for soldiers, and Rose was doing something to her fingernails. I sat in the corner and scratched away. My pen nib's twisted, so it wasn't very neat.

'What are you doing, Fred?' Mum asked.

'Writing,' I said.

Rose looked up. 'Don't be cheeky.'

Honestly! What's cheeky about telling the truth?

Mum said, 'Are you writing to Orris again?'

Luckily, at that point, Dad burst out laughing and spilled his tea on his trousers, so they forgot about me.

Auntie Vi came this afternoon. She's fun, but I hardly ever see her, because she lives so far away. I was off out with my cart when she clacked along the road in her high heels, yelling, 'Yoo-hoo, Fred! Give us a hand with this, will you?'

I carried her packages upstairs. She asked what I was doing, so I told her about salvaging and helping people.

Auntie Vi had a bag of cakes – I could smell them – so I stayed until I was offered one. She's got a great job, working with the huge barrage balloons that fly over London. Well, they don't fly – they're tethered to the ground, but they look like they're flying. Auntie Vi reckons it's her and her team of girls (she's the captain) who'll keep London safe when the German planes come.

'We'll stop them coming in low and shooting you,' she said. That was a horrible thought. She smiled sweetly at Mum. 'In return, please could I have a bath – just a little one?'

'Of course, love,' said Mum.

'Why d'you want a bath?' I asked, partly out of
nosiness, but partly because she hadn't got the
cakes out, and I wanted to remind her I was still
there.

'Our balloons are on the green in front of
some houses,' said Auntie Vi. 'The government
pays the house owners to let us have a bath, but
today they're either out or haven't got any hot

water, and I've got a date tonight.' She laughed. 'When we joined up, they told us, "Don't worry – you can bath in a bucket of water."' She winked. 'I'm not about to try!'

I snorted. Even Mum giggled at the thought of Auntie Vi trying to squeeze into a bucket.

I gave up. 'I'm off on my rounds, then.'

She picked up her package – I suppose it was her bath stuff – and the cakes. 'This is my real payment for the bath – catch!' And she tossed the bag to me!

'Thanks!' I said.

'You deserve it,' she said, disappearing into the bathroom. 'Now you're a cog.'

'What's a cog?' I called, but she'd shut the door.

I looked at Mum. She shrugged.

Yesterday was one of my best days ever. I'm now collecting metal, as well as rags and paper. You don't get many rags, because people use material to make something else. Mum made me a jacket out of one of Dad's that had worn too thin for the office. It's horrible. I always take it off when I'm out of sight.

When I got home, Mum said, 'I've got two bits of news. Berry had a chat with Auntie Vi, and she's going to join the WAAF –'

'The what?'

'The Women's Auxiliary Air Force,' said Mum. 'The ones who do the balloons. Berry's going to join.'

Flip. I never thought of Berry as grown up. Perhaps Rose will join.

'The other news,' said Mum, 'is about the Cogs. You can join!'

'What is it?' I asked. I want to do my bit, but not if it's dangerous.

'You're doing it already,' she said. 'The Women's Voluntary Service run Cogs. It's for children who want to be a cog in the wheel – that means a small part of the big war effort. Cogs collect salvage. The WVS weigh it and you earn a badge, and a rank, like in the army.'

That's for ME! I wish I'd kept today's load instead of taking it down the Cubs. But tomorrow I'll take a new lot to the WVS collection point.

This Cogs thing is wizard! They gave me an orangey-red badge – it's round, with a cog inside it – and said I'm Private Frederick Barrow. This is more like it!

I've collected nearly a full cart-load each day. Some of the neighbours have started bringing salvage stuff round to our flat now. It saves me calling at inconvenient times, they said.

Mum doesn't want it in the house, so I built a sort of lean-to against the fence at the bottom of the garden. It does lean, too. It's wobbly, but it keeps the stuff dry.

The WVS lady said today, 'You must have a

whole team of young chaps working for you! You'll be Corporal Barrow in no time!'

I said I collect on my own, but I could see she didn't believe me. Didn't matter. It gave me an idea.

I'm going to get this salvaging thing organised. I'll be the Lone Salvager no more!

I've got Jeffrey, John, Clifford and Colin all in Cogs now, and they've all got badges. We go collecting separately after school, and bring the stuff

back to my garden. We've made my lean-to stronger and bigger. On Saturdays we load it on our carts and wheelbarrows and take it to the WVS. The lady weighs it and divides it by five, so we each get a share on our record. Once we got an old mangle – that was good and heavy!

I've also organised the house. Mrs Little and Mum have to put their stuff for salvage in separate piles in the hall. I've made a list of what everything's for, to encourage them. There's tins, anything made of aluminium to help make aircraft and books for soldiers. Also paper to make cartridge wads, and to be turned into new paper, and jam jars (don't know what they're for, but the WVS want them – perhaps it's for jam). I need old clothes, cotton reels, knitting wool, Dad's used razor blades (Mum insists they go in a jam jar, for safety's sake, which messes up my organisation) and saucepans. I've only ever had one saucepan, and that had a hole in it. I also collect bones, which make glue for aeroplanes, and they make

glycerine, which is used in explosives!

Uncle Jim's saving bones from his shop. There aren't many, because his customers like boiling bones up for stock or something, or soup. I'd hate to find a bone in my soup.

'They can't eat the bones, though,' I said. 'Can't they give them back to you when they've done the soup?'

He laughed.

I saw a notice today saying housewives can manage with one saucepan. Mum said she's got three and if I touch them they won't need glycerine to make her explode.

I really am doing my bit! The WVS ladies cheer when they see me coming. It's good to be helping the war, not that we've seen much of it. There's sandbags everywhere, and the blackout, and Mum moans about rationing, but there's no shooting or bombs. Perhaps there won't be. Perhaps it'll just be our soldiers shooting it out with German ones.

Dad says the neighbours think I'm overdoing it a bit. The woman over the back complained about the bones in my salvage shelter. She says they smell and attract flies. I'd have thought she'd be glad the flies were on my bones and not in her garden.

Another neighbour says I'm always asking for their newspapers before they've read them.

One woman said she feels guilty if she puts more than one pan on the stove, and she doesn't think a little boy should make her feel like that. Huh!

Dad said, 'I've got something else for you to do, to take your mind off salvaging for an hour a day.'

He's bought five hens. If Mum gives up our egg ration, we can get chicken feed instead, and have fresh eggs.

'Uncle Ken said you know about chickens,' said Dad.

Well, I chucked food at them and collected the eggs, so I suppose I do. But it won't stop me salvaging. That's more important.

↬ ↬ ↬

Big trouble today. The woman who did the money in Uncle Jim's shop has gone away, so Auntie Joan's helping out. Today Mrs Little, who's known Auntie Joan since they were little (ha ha), was in there, and Auntie Joan gave her a lump of ham. They probably wrapped it under the counter so no one else saw, because ham's rationed.

This evening, I was doing the chickens when I heard Berry's voice calling me from the Littles' flat. I went in, stepping over a pile of shoes and a box of Christmas decorations, and said, 'What on earth are you doing here?'

'I'm on leave for two days. I passed my tests and did a lot of marching and training and now I'm on the balloons.'

'D'you like it?' I asked.

'It's hard work,' she said, 'but the girls are ever so much fun. Oh, Freddy, I've missed you.'

As she hugged me, I looked over her shoulder. Amongst the clutter and rubble littering Mrs Little's table, there was a plate piled with sliced ham, and another with the ham bone on it.

I wanted that bone. To me it became a pot of glue, holding a British fighter plane together.

'That looks nice ham,' I began.

'Big eyes!' Berry picked up a small slice and popped it in my mouth, then put the plate in the meat safe.

'Berr-eeee!' came Mrs Little's voice. 'You put my hat on the top hook – I can't reach it!'

'Coming, Mum,' called Berry. 'Fred, I'll pop up to see you before I go back.'

Once she'd left the kitchen, I grabbed the ham bone and legged it to my salvage shelter. Mrs Little would never miss it in all that mess.

Wrong.

Twenty minutes later, she clattered up the stairs. 'Where's that boy?' she demanded.

'In the living room,' Mum said calmly.

I wiped my hands on the armchair, in case they smelled of ham.

Mrs Little burst in. 'You took my bone!' she said. 'I'd promised that to my cousin for her mother who's got no teeth!'

Stupidly, instead of saying, 'What bone?' I

said, 'What good's a bone to someone with no teeth?'

Mum was tight-lipped.

'You make soup with it, you silly boy,' Mrs Little said. 'Now where's my bone?'

'I'll fetch it.' I went down and got the bone. I wanted to tell her that one of our brave fighter pilots would be flying a plane that wasn't stuck together properly, all because she wanted her bone back. I wiped it off with my hanky.

Mrs Little took her bone, and said to Mum, 'Can't stop, Pearl. I've got some clearing-up to do.'

She'd need an army tank to clear up her flat. Old bat, stopping a boy from helping to win the war.

Mum warned me about upsetting people. 'Everybody's got enough to worry about with all the rationing and everything,' she said.

Dad made me listen to Mr Churchill's speech today. He's our new Prime Minister. Dad says if anyone can win this war, Mr Churchill can.

Well, he can't win it by himself, can he? So we've all still got to do our bit. Especially now the Germans have beaten Belgium and France.

Dad went to the Cup Final with some office friends, and he didn't take me! He came home all excited and reeking of beer.

'Why didn't you take me?' I asked. 'You promised you'd take me to the next Cup Final!'

'Ah, that's the real Cup Final,' he said. 'They're not having it this year.'

'I know,' I said, 'they're having the War Cup, but it was still a cup final, and it was West Ham!'

He got cross. 'I didn't even know I was going until I got to the office,' he said. 'I could hardly come home and get you, could I?'

Well, yes.

'West Ham won,' he said. 'That should please you.'

It's not the point.

Something amazing's happened! Everyone's going on about it. Thousands of our soldiers were trapped on the French coast at a place called Dunkirk. Just about anyone who has a boat went across the English Channel to rescue them. There were ferries and fishing boats – all sorts, big and little, hundreds of them. Because they were small, they could get in close to the beach. The soldiers must have been so glad to see them.

All the Germans have got to do now is cross the sea to England, and we're next. We need more bullets and planes and guns. I must collect more salvage!

The sirens went off at one o'clock this morning. I grabbed Eric and yelled for Mum. She and Dad were outside the bedroom throwing on dressing gowns. Rose appeared with her hair in pins and a net, and her face all slimy with cream. She looked *dreadful*!

'No!' she wailed. 'Don't tell me we're going into that black hole of a shelter – not in the middle of the night!'

'Shut up, Rose,' said Dad. 'Help your mother.'

Mum dragged a couple of blankets off her bed. I couldn't find my shoes, so I put slippers on and hoped it wouldn't be muddy.

It was.

The siren was still wailing, which was good, because it drowned out Rose's whining. We followed Dad and the faint torchlight glow on his feet, and went down into the shelter and sat on the benches, getting our breath back. My heart pounded so loud I thought everyone would hear it.

Mum poked her head out of the door. 'Where's Mrs Little?' she said anxiously.

'I'm here,' said a small voice from the corner.

Rose screamed!

It was Mrs Little! She was so small and huddled I'd thought she was a heap of blankets.

She was in tears. 'What about my Berry? Oh, Pearl, will my Berry be all right?'

Dad lit the lamp. Mum swapped places with Rose, and hugged Mrs Little. 'She'll be fine. She's got those great barrage balloons above – that'll stop any German planes getting near her. And she's near an anti-aircraft emplacement, isn't she? No harm's going to come to her.'

I wasn't so sure. If I was a German pilot, and I saw ack-ack guns firing up at me, that's exactly where I'd drop my bombs.

I waited, dreading that any moment I'd hear enemy planes. My stomach felt like two big fists were squeezing it.

Suddenly Rose screamed again. 'Spider!'

I jumped up. 'OK, Rose – I'll find one for you!'

She'd have throttled me if Mum hadn't held her back.

We were there till four this morning. I read all the comics we'd stored in there, then I hummed till everyone told me to stop. I never heard a plane, or an explosion, never heard gunfire.

What I did hear was Mrs Little, upset, which upset me a bit, too. It made me realise how much I like Berry.

Rose sat with her feet on the bench, in case a creepy-crawly crept up her leg. We had one more scream when I scratched Eric's ears and his wagging tail touched her ankle.

When the all-clear went, it was getting light.

Well, I don't know what that was all about.

✈ ✈ ✈

Mum and Rose are both in a bad mood. Mum says it's hard enough to cope with rationing, and not being able to get certain food, but now they're rationing tea.

'How will I cope without my cuppa?' she grumbled.

'I know,' Rose wailed. 'And d'you know what else? They want us to wear flat shoes instead of high heels – to save on wood! I ask you, how much wood is there in a shoe heel? Barely a twig's worth! Me wearing flat shoes won't win the war, will it?'

She makes me wild. 'Rose,' I said, 'if all the women in the country wore flat shoes –'

'Oh, shut up!' she stormed. 'What does a little squirt like you know about it?'

I know a lot more than she does.

✈ ✈ ✈

I noticed lots of women wearing high heels today, so I mentioned to some of them about saving wood. A few were really nice. One woman said, 'I'll finish wearing these shoes out, because we mustn't waste, but then I'll buy flat ones.'

Another one said, 'Good to see a young person being so conscientious.'

'Just doing my bit,' I said.

A woman down the market said, 'Mind your

own business,' and told me where to go. Not very ladylike, that one!

When I told Mum what I'd been doing, she said why not stick to what I know best – salvage work. Rose pushed past me on her way to cream her face

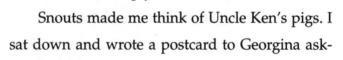

and said, 'Yes. Keep your snout – out!'

Snouts made me think of Uncle Ken's pigs. I sat down and wrote a postcard to Georgina asking how they were.

Rose has got a job! It's in the office of a factory. I heard Dad tell Mum he doesn't know how long she'll last. I asked Rose what the factory makes and she said it's top secret and highly dangerous. I thought it must be bullets, or even bombs, but

Mum said it's just instruments for aircrafts.

The nice thing is, it's school holidays, and she won't be around! Not that I'm ever indoors. I'm either walking Eric, feeding chickens, queuing to buy something for Mum, or doing my bit for the war effort.

They've had bombs dropped in places near the coast. Maybe that's as far as the Germans will get. Doesn't matter how far they get, we still have to go to the shelter.

I've got a job, too! Uncle Jim says his delivery boy's gone off to the war, and he can't use the van because petrol – when he can get it – is about two bob a gallon. I'm to run errands for him on a butcher's bike, and he'll pay me! Hope it's not in chops or liver.

When I got home, there was a letter from Georgina. She'd put a note in it from Orris, only she put Horace.

The pigs are well, and the little ones have

grown up. 'We've just had a litter of twelve fine porkers,' she wrote. 'They're all healthy – just one runt. But don't you worry, my friend. I'll care for it and see it has a fair share of feed. I'm enclosing an epistle written by my newest companion, Horace. Thanks to your intervention, he's left Miss White, and now dwells happily with Ken and Dot. Well done, old chap.'

She didn't mention Mickey, Goofy or Donald. I hope they're all right.

> Deer Fred fank you for getting me to leev Miss Wits and cum ear. Im very appy ear. I like it ear even the cows. May be il see you agin wun day.
>
> From yo're frend Horace

I'm happy I helped Orris.

I asked Dad what a runt was. He said it's a weak piglet, who gets pushed out by the others at feeding time, and sometimes doesn't live. Aah. Poor little things. I sat and thought about the farm and the pigs and everything, and had a sudden brainwave. I already collect paper, metal, wool, string, bones and other stuff. The one thing I haven't done anything about is pig swill. Uncle Jim rents a bit of land from someone near the common, and he keeps pigs. He'd like some swill, I'll bet.

There's a whole world of pigs in London, and I didn't know it! Uncle Jim told me lots of people belong to pig clubs. They put their money together to buy a pig, and one of them keeps it – in his garden, I suppose. They all get food for it – not just pig swill, but proper feed, too. I like that idea.

Uncle Jim said he'll be glad of fresh pig swill. Well, I'll start right here at home. I'll get a clean bucket, and Mum can put all her trimmings in it, and we can scrape our plates into it. I'll put another one downstairs for Mrs Little, and I'll tell all the neighbours that I'll collect all their peelings and stuff every day. Then I'll take it to Uncle Jim and he'll boil it up for his pigs.

I've found some elderly people who keep pigs, and they live just next to the common. I never knew they were there, but Mum says you can smell them when the wind's right. She meant the pigs, not the people. The man's called Len, and he says he'd love some extra feed.

There's been lots more bombing. Wales have had it, and Scotland, and down in the southwest. It's strange to think of the beach we go to in Devon with barbed wire on it, to stop spies sneaking ashore like smugglers of olden days.

Here in London, it all looks the same, except for the barrage balloons, and the sandbags packed against buildings. And the blackout at night. And the ARP notices. And the posters saying don't spread rumours, and to 'Dig for Victory' and to eat carrots and so on. No, it doesn't look the same at all, really.

I took a huge load of pig swill round to Len and Kath – that's his wife. They let me help with the pigs sometimes, but they were going out today, so I just watched them for a bit, and gave them a scratch (the pigs, not Len and Kath!) When I started all this salvage lark, I said I was going to do my bit by becoming the champion salvager, and by helping people while I did my rounds. Len and Kath need help, so I'll make sure they're never short of swill.

The Germans have been shooting at England with huge guns from the other side of the Channel. They've smashed four houses in Dover.

We keep hearing reports that the RAF have shot down lots of German planes. Nearly eighty, Dad said, a couple of days ago. They've shot down some of ours, but not as many. Mum made rock cakes today, so I asked for two to take to Len and Kath tomorrow. She said, 'Yes, as long as you don't feed them to the pigs.' I wouldn't do that. I've put them in my jacket pocket, and I don't think I'll be able to sleep, knowing they're in the room.

This morning, Mum and Dad told me that Mum's expecting a baby. Honestly, any fool could see that. But it was only afterwards that I suddenly twigged that she's expecting a *baby*. I mean, at first it was just a word, but it's real now. I'm going to have a little brother. I hope it's a brother. Dad said I must help Mum and not worry her. They want to tell Rose to be helpful, not me.

I've just had an awful thought. When Mum goes into hospital, Rose'll be looking after us.

Mrs Little knows. She keeps popping upstairs to offer to do things, like ironing. Mum won't let her anywhere near our iron. All Mrs

Little's clothes are as creased as old apples.

I ate the rock cakes. Well, it thundered all night, and I couldn't sleep. There wasn't anything else to do.

Everyone thinks Hitler's going to start bombing London soon. Mum was in tears today. Mrs Little stopped me when I went down for the milk, and said, 'Keep an eye on Mum, Fred. She doesn't like the heat, not in her – you know.' She meant her condition.

Before Rose went to work, she hugged Mum and said, 'Don't worry. Our boys will sort Hitler out, you'll see.'

'But the baby, Rose,' said Mum. 'What sort of a world is this to bring a child into? Everyone anxious and frightened . . . bombs about to fall . . .' She began to sob. I went over, and me and Rose cuddled her. Rose smiled at me. I smiled back.

Afterwards, Rose said, 'She'll be all right, Fred. We all will.'

Blimey, she's changed.

+ + +

We've had a horrible few days. The sirens keep going, and yesterday, in the shelter, I heard planes go over. Mum clutched her tummy and her eyes were all watery. Mrs Little screwed herself up into a ball and prayed. She was probably praying for Berry, so I said one, too. Rose put her arm round Mum and was all grown up, but she still complained about earwigs and stuff.

Last night I heard explosions. They were a long way away.

Portsmouth got bombed. Dad said it was

really bad, but yesterday we shot down nearly eighty German planes. Plenty of them get through, though – they've been bombing our airfields and factories.

I'm only allowed out for a bit at a time. Mum's scared I'll be stuck somewhere when the sirens go. She likes us all together. It's rotten, because I can't meet John and Jeffrey, or get to the WVS ladies. I've been saving up pig swill, though, for Len and Kath.

Rose was out with Skinny Lynnie the other night when the siren went. Mum nearly went berserk until she turned up in the morning, safe and sound.

'We went down the underground station,' Rose said between hugs from Mum. 'Loads of people did. Some of them have started going down there every night, because they feel safe there. We had a sing-song and chatted, ever so friendly-like. It was fun!'

I thought Mum would hit the ceiling. 'Fun?

Fun! I was worried sick!'

Flip. One minute Rose was hugged and kissed, the next she was bellowed at. Grown-ups!

✈ ✈ ✈

Berry called in today. She said it's her last leave for a bit, because Hitler says he's going to give us what-for. 'We'll be ready for him,' she said. 'Don't you worry, young Freddy.'

She gave Mum a little white woolly thing she's knitted for the baby. I couldn't speak for a minute. Imagine something that small! It'll be my baby brother – or sister. Mum said it'll be born in a few weeks.

✈ ✈ ✈

They sprang a surprise on me today. Not a surprise. A shock. They want me out of London again, because the bombing's going to get bad. I'm being evacuated tomorrow.

'John and Jeffrey are going in a day or two,' Mum said, 'and Colin and Clifford went yesterday. It'll be safer for you.'

'Can't we all go?' I asked.

Dad explained that everyone in his department must stay. 'You keep saying how important it is for you to do your bit, Fred,' he said. 'This is the way I do mine. It's war work.'

'But what about Mum?'

He said Mum flatly refuses to leave him. 'And Rose will be needed to help Mum. Who's going to wash my shirts when Mum has the baby, eh?'

'But I want to see the baby!'

Rose put her arm round me. 'It'll probably all be over by then,' she said. 'We'll wipe Hitler's bombers right out of the sky, see if we don't.'

I asked Mum if she had a letter or anything for Auntie Dot.

She looked at Dad and bit her lip. 'Sorry, Fred,' she said. 'Dot's not well, so you can't go to the farm. You'll go to someone new, and I know you'll have a lovely time. It's not a huge distance from London. Dad will get the train up to visit you one weekend soon.'

I didn't want to go, but because I know what being evacuated's like, I'm not worried.

I had to deliver all the salvage left in my lean-to, and say goodbye to Len and Kath and the pigs. When I went down to pick up my pig swill buckets, they'd gone!

'Mrs Little!' I shouted. 'Have you seen –'

She beetled out of her kitchen. 'I didn't need to see it,' she said, 'I could smell it! It's outside the front door. You could gas the whole German army with that stink!'

Len and Kath were sad to see me go, but said it's best for me. I had one last look round – there was a new litter that would need feeding. Len showed me one he was worried about. It had a funny ear, shaped like India upside down.

'A runt, is it?' I asked.

100

He nodded.

'Poor thing,' I said. If I was staying, I'd have given it extra feed. 'Promise you'll look after it?' I asked.

Len nodded. 'Course we will. We'll call it Fred if you like.'

Bit embarrassing! 'No!' I said. Then I remembered the first time I'd heard of runts. 'Call it Georgina,' I suggested.

Len laughed. 'It's a boy!'

'Better make it George, then,' said Kath. That seemed to suit it.

'Sorry I can't bring swill any more,' I said, 'but I will when I come back.'

They didn't say anything more, just waved goodbye.

✈ ✈ ✈

This morning, my case and gas mask were ready, I had my ration book, clean hanky and a packet of sandwiches. A woman was coming in a car to take me to the train, and someone else would look after me on the way. We said goodbye before she came, because Mum said she'd be in a rush.

She was! In no time, I was in the car, waving to my mum and my dad and my sister, and even Mrs Little, who's not keen on boys. My eyes were so full of tears I was afraid to blink in case they spilled. There were two other kids in the car and they both looked as miserable as I felt.

Then it was the train – hot, stuffy and packed.

There were kids of all sizes, and mothers with children, as well as the woman who was looking after us. I shared my sandwiches with a girl, and she gave me an apple. She said it was from her tree and she'd got loads. We had labels on our coats. I felt like a squashed parcel.

When we arrived, there were people every-where, and we didn't know what was happening. I sat on the ground and watched while people came up and took kids. Eventually the woman who looked after us said, 'Here we are, Miss Jordan, you'll be taking –' She looked at my label. 'You'll be taking Frederick Barrow.'

Miss Jordan looked down at me. 'If I have to have one, I'd rather have a girl,' she said.

The woman smiled and shrugged. 'I'm sorry . . .'

Miss Jordan didn't smile. 'Come along then,' she said to me, 'and pick your feet up.'

I hadn't even taken a step.

We got to her house which smells of polish and is dark because the curtains are never fully opened. Miss Jordan's got a father who leaves his false teeth in a glass of water all the time.

'Well, Frederick,' he said, 'brought your ration book, have you? If you haven't, you'll get nothing to eat here.' And he went 'Tee hee', just like they do in comics.

It's awful here. My bed is hard, there's nothing to read and nothing to do. The only building nearby is the station, half a mile away. If you want to get to houses and shops, you have to cross the railway track and walk about another mile. There's a joined-on house next door, but it's empty. There isn't even a cat.

Miss Jordan never talks, and all her father says is, 'Gwen, bring me this,' or 'Gwen, I want that.'

Worst of all, she checks my bed every morning to make sure I haven't wet it. It makes me so mad. I was three last time that happened! Well, I might have had a little accident once or twice since then, but Miss Jordan's got me so worried that I have to go to the toilet about five times before I can get to sleep. My mum wouldn't take any notice if I wet the bed. I mean, she'd change the sheets, of course, but she wouldn't get cross. She understands, my mum does. 'These things happen,' she says.

But Miss Jordan would probably hang the sheets on the line with a notice saying, 'Fred Barrow wet the bed. I knew he would.'

I can't stand it here. When I wrote back to Mum and Dad today, I asked to come home. I didn't say how really miserable I am, because a teacher at the school I go to said that upsets your parents, and it's not helpful.

Miss Jordan reads the newspaper to her father. Her voice is all on one note except when she gets to the end of a sentence. Then it tails off downwards, like the air-raid siren.

We had tripe casserole for dinner. It's the most disgusting thing you could ever imagine eating, if you don't count spiders and maggots. I wouldn't even feed it to Eric. When I asked Miss Jordan what tripe was, she got as far as talking about cows' stomachs and I had to leave the table. I had a big lump of it in my mouth and I thought I was going to be sick. I certainly couldn't swallow it. She sent me to my room and said, 'Come down later when you're really hungry.' If I did she'd probably put it in front of me again.

Thinking about Eric made me sad. I wonder if anyone's taking him for walks.

No letter from Mum and Dad. I'm so fed up. I cried in bed last night. I miss home. I miss being kissed goodnight.

The school's all right. There are too many of us to fit in it, so we have some lessons in the village hall, which smells of old plimsolls. The teachers are nice, but ever so strict, and they keep getting our names muddled. Each day we have one or two new kids, and lots of us are homesick. I haven't made any special friends. There's no point. No one would ever be allowed to come and play where I'm staying, and Miss Jordan won't let me out after school, except in the garden. 'I'm responsible for you,' she says, 'and if you're roaming the streets, anything might happen to you.' Flip, if someone said hello it would be more exciting than staying here.

The garden's a real danger zone, because the flowers are planted in rows, and stand up straight like soldiers. You wouldn't dare kick a ball in it – if you even had a ball.

I got a letter today. I haven't stopped crying since I opened it. Mum's in hospital, and she's had the baby. I've got a little brother and I can't even see him. All the others can see him, but I have to stay in this hateful, dark, miserable house all on my own.

Later

I went downstairs and told Miss Jordan I've got a new baby brother. She said, 'That's nice. Pass me the floor polish, please.'

So I went outside, where Mr Jordan was tying big flowers to sticks. I said, 'I've got a new baby brother.'

'Have you now,' he said, but it wasn't really a question.

'Yes. I wish I could see him.'

'Well, let's hope he doesn't get hurt with all those bombs, eh?'

I don't think he meant to frighten me, but he did. All the news is full of bombs and air raids and Hitler's Blitz on London, and I'm worried about my family. I want to be with them.

And I'm going to. I'm going home. I don't know how, but I am. I've got some money from when I worked for Uncle Jim – not much, but enough for some food on the way.

🛩 🛩 🛩

After school today, I chatted to the station-master. All the time we were talking, I was finding out information about the trains to London. They're not written up anywhere, in case a German spy wants to find his way around.

He gave me some bread and honey, and asked how it is at Miss Jordan's. I shrugged and pretended my mouth was too full to answer.

When I'd found out what I needed, I said goodbye.

He tilted his cap up and looked at me closely. 'You ask a lot of questions, young man. You're not a spy, are you?'

'Do I look like one?'

'No,' he said, 'but you might be in disguise.'
Then he laughed. 'Run along with you. Oh, wait!'
He went into his office and brought out a comic.
'Someone left this behind. I was going to take it
home for my boy, but I reckon you need cheering
up more than he does.'

In bed that night, I read that comic over and
over. Then I got up early next morning, packed
my case, got my gas mask and left a note on the
dining table. It said, 'I've gone home to see my
family. Thank you for having me. Frederick.'

I was looking forward to being Fred again.

Getting away was much easier than I expected. I
waited behind the station house until the train
came in then, while the stationmaster spoke to the
guard, I opened a door and jumped in. The carriage had a corridor and a toilet. I didn't sit down
straight away in case someone asked where my
mum was. Every time someone came into the cor-

ridor, I locked myself in the toilet in case I was asked to show my ticket. No one bothered me, except a woman who said, 'You've been standing alone for quite a while, young man. Are you travelling by yourself?'

'No,' I said. 'I'm with my mum and my brothers and sisters, but they're sitting further along. I came here because it's quieter and I want to look out of the window. The baby keeps crying.'

She smiled. And blow me down, just then, a man came along saying, 'Tickets, please.' Trapped, I thought!

The woman showed him hers, and he said, 'What about you, young man?'

I didn't know what to say, so I just looked at him. Then the woman said, 'His family are further along. His mother will have his ticket.'

He believed her!

I didn't want to stay talking, so I found a seat and read the comic the stationmaster gave me – again. I can't wait to get back to salvaging. I'll have plenty to read then.

When we got off the train in London, there was a barrier, and I couldn't see how to get past the ticket collector. I hid in among a bunch of people, but I could see the ticket collector was checking everyone carefully.

Then, on the far side of the barrier, I spotted a woman with a whole bunch of kids, walking towards the exit.

I ran to the barrier, pointing and shouting, 'There's my mum! She's gone without me! Let me through! Mum!'

The ticket collector blocked my way. 'Hold up, sonny,' he said. 'Where's your ticket?'

'My mum had it! She gave it to you – I saw her! I got left behind in the crowd! Quick – she hasn't noticed I'm missing – lemme catch her up!'

'Let him go through,' said the woman from the train. 'He was definitely with his mother – I can vouch for that.'

'Yes, let him through,' said another woman.

'Quickly,' said a soldier, 'he'll never catch her up if you keep him here any longer.'

And the ticket collector let me through! My legs shook and I felt nearly as sick as when I had a mouthful of tripe.

That reminded me, I needed something to eat. And then I realised I'd done something dreadful. I'd left my ration book at Miss Jordan's. I didn't know what I could buy without a ration book, so I decided to get the bus and get home as quickly as possible. In the toilets I found a tap marked, 'Drinking water', and tried to fill up with that. But all it did was make me burp, and I still felt hungry.

When I got off the bus and turned the corner, I couldn't believe it was my road. If I hadn't seen our house still standing, I would have stood and screamed. Three houses on the opposite side had been bombed into heaps of rubble, and the one next to ours had been hit as well. One whole side was gone and there, upstairs, as if someone had put

it on a giant shelf, was their bath! The wallpaper was hanging off, and curtains, all tattered, blew in the breeze. The blackout material was shredded. Oh, blimey, I thought, I hope they were in the shelter when the bomb hit.

I ran to our house. One side of the steps up to the front door was missing. There was just a pile of bricks beside it. I banged on the door. One, two, three!

The door opened, and there was my mum. She stared at me, then held out her arms.

'Fred! Oh, my Fred! What have you done! Are you all right?'

I nodded. 'But Mum, it was so horrible at Miss Jordan's. I wanted you, and I was so lonely and I've forgotten my ration book. Please don't send me away again. I'll stay in the shelter all night if you want, then I'll be safe here with all of you.'

Through my tears, I saw Mrs Little nearby, shaking her head. I couldn't hear it, but I bet her tongue was tutting.

Mum pulled me upstairs. Eric was so excited to see me that he did a wee up the wall. Mum gave me a cup of tea and we talked until it was time for her to start Dad's dinner.

How could I have forgotten? 'Mum!' I said. 'Where's the baby?'

She nodded towards her bedroom. 'In there. Go and see.'

In a cot, lying on his side facing the wall, was my brother. He had a bit of hair, and he kept snuffling.

I felt a hand on my shoulder. It was Dad. I started to explain, but he said, 'I know. Don't worry any more. What do you think of Number Two Son?'

'Eh?'

'Well, you're our Number One Son,' said Dad, which made me feel special. 'So he's Number Two.'

'What's his real name?' I asked.

The poor little thing hasn't got one! They can't decide!

When Rose came home from work and got over the shock of seeing me, she got Number Two up, and changed his nappy. It was awful. I'll keep out of the way whenever that happens. I'd rather muck out a pig sty.

At dinner time, Mum said she wants us all to stay together. 'I can't bear it without all my family under one roof,' she said.

So it was just as bad for her when I was away as it was for me. Except she didn't have to eat tripe.

✈ ✈ ✈

I slept for about an hour and a half last night, before the sirens went off. Down we all went to the shelter. It's better organised now. There's books, a pack of cards and two lamps. Rose and Mum took knitting, and practically every five minutes Mrs Little said a prayer to St Bernadette (that's Berry's proper name – she's Berry for short). Mum got fed up and gave her some bread and jam – no butter – to keep her mouth busy. The jam was nice, but not as sweet as I like.

There was a lot of noise outside. When planes came towards us, I could hear the engines growl. As they came closer, the growl rumbled in my tummy. There were several dull thuds, and everyone looked at each other. We knew they were bombs exploding.

Damp, chilly, smelly, scary – I was just happy to be back with my family. We all took turns cuddling Number Two, to keep him warm, and we put the lamps out while Mum fed him. He's so sweet. I can't wait for him to grow a bit. He doesn't do much at the moment.

When the all-clear went, we came out to find the sky streaked with smoke and, in the distance, the glow of fires.

'Will they bomb our street again?' I asked.

'They'll bomb wherever they want,' Rose said. 'Lynn's cousin's house was bombed to smithereens one night. Three nights later, another one landed in exactly the same place.'

I looked at next door, standing like a ruined castle against the dawn sky.

Dad put an arm round me. 'I always believe lightning never strikes twice in the same place.'

We went back to bed.

Len and Kath have gone. Some people down the road said they'd decided to get away from London.

'What about their animals?' I asked, but the people didn't know.

I went round the back of Len's house and down the garden. Someone else must have been in, because all the fruit had been stripped off the bushes, and there wasn't much left growing that could still be eaten.

The sties were empty. I wandered down to the orchard. The grass was long and everywhere looked wild. The apples had been picked – there were just a few at the very tops of the trees. I shook a branch, and two or three fell down. I caught one, and the others landed and rolled away.

Suddenly, something pink shot past me, straight for the apples. It was a pig! As it was snuffling and munching, I noticed a funny-shaped ear. India upside down!

'George?' I said. I edged forward and scratched his back. Then I gave him my apple.

'Come on,' I said. 'Let's take a look at your sty.' I picked George up. He was still very small, and quite happy to be handled. Len and Kath obviously kept their promise to look after him.

I checked the sty. It was OK, but pretty filthy, even for a pig. I got water from the rain barrel for George and left him drinking. I needed to pee, so I went to the outside toilet. As I shut the door I noticed a note nailed to it. Written on the outside was, 'To Fred, the pig swill boy.'

I pulled it off.

Dear Fred, We've gone to stay with Kath's people near Exeter. The pigs had to go to the butcher, but we kept our promise about George. All we can do is let him loose. He'll forage for himself — there's plenty to dig up in our garden — and we've left lots of containers around to catch rain water. If the worst comes to the worst, he can always drink the pond! He'll be a happy pig and, who knows, maybe Hitler will soon get what's coming to him, and you'll come home. We know you'll see that George is all right.

Best wishes to you. You're a good lad.

Len and Kath

I picked up George and headed home. After a bit, I slowed down. What would Mum say? I tried to picture a pig in our flat. It would probably be perfectly at home in Mrs Little's, but not in ours.

Then I had a brainwave.

🛩 🛩 🛩

George has a new home! It's the air-raid shelter in the back garden of the bombed-out house next door. There's no one to shelter in it, so it might as well be useful. I took the door off and fixed a piece of fencing across, so there's lots of light and air getting in.

The garden wall's down in several places, so it's easy to slip next door. You have to watch your step climbing over the rubble, but that's no problem.

Feeding George isn't a problem, either – after all, aren't I the king of pig swill? Just have to hog it all for myself now.

🛩 🛩 🛩

No one's mentioned school yet, so I went back on my rounds today. It's a shame Jeffrey and the others are still evacuated, but it doesn't really matter. I'm not giving up.

Anyway, lots of my regular people were pleased to see me. I just had one or two instances of, 'Oh you're back to nag us, are you?' and 'I remember you – you're the one who practically pulled my milk pan out of my hands.'

I collected stuff for swill, put it in my salvage shelter and waited for Mum to go out. She takes ages at the shops these days, because of the queuing.

Once she'd gone, I got my swill and began to boil it up. It took for ever, because you can only get so much in a pan at one time, otherwise it boils over and makes a horrible mess.

When Mum came home, she sniffed. 'What's that smell? Is that you? What have you been doing?'

She was not happy.

But somebody was – George! I took him round a bucketful this evening. Tomorrow I'll get up extra early and let him out for a good run round. There's a part of next door's garden that can't be seen from our house because of a big holly tree. I'll fence off a bit so George can be outside in the daytime. If I let him out whenever I can, he'll grow big and healthy.

I got a letter from Georgina and Orris in the evening post! It's in two bits. First there's all Georgina's news about the farm, and especially the pigs which she calls 'magnificent brutes'. Then there's a bit from Orris. His spelling's improved.

Miss Wites bin stuck wiv too more kids and there runnin her raggid. Yo're Arnty Dot says I'm an appy addishon to the farm an I kin stay as long as I wonts. I'm glad yoo got me ear Fred.

From Horace

I showed Mum and she said when the war's over, perhaps Orris can come and stay with us. But first, I'm going to write and tell him and Georgina that I'm a pig farmer now – sort of!

⤴ ⤴ ⤴

Yesterday evening began normally. Dad was working late. 'If the raids are bad,' he'd said, 'I'll stay at the office.'

Mum wanted to visit Mrs Wilson three doors up – she's had an operation, and Mum says she's starved of company.

I got my book out. Rose was in charge, as usual, and I could hear Mum in the kitchen, telling her what to do and what not to do. Then she came in to say goodbye. 'I'll only be an hour or so,' she said. 'I'll be back well before Hitler disturbs the night.'

She kissed me, and said, 'I love you. Never forget.' She says that every time she goes out nowadays.

Rose listened to the wireless, then went to her

bedroom to fiddle with make-up, and moon over her film star pictures. My book was The Children of the New Forest. It's about some kids who lived in secret, in a forest, during a war hundreds of years ago. It's quite exciting, and when the air-raid siren went, I grabbed it and set off down-stairs, with Rose not far behind, and Eric barking at the excitement.

I stopped suddenly. 'What about Mum?'

Rose pushed me. 'She'll go to Mrs Wilson's shelter,' she snapped. 'Quick! I can hear the planes already!'

I thought they were probably our planes, but I didn't argue. It was really dark, and Rose had forgotten the torch, so we clutched each other as we made our way down to the shelter. Mrs Little was already there, muttering away. Rose tried to light the lamps. She made a mess of it, so I snatched the matches from her. It was getting noisy outside, and it felt as if the ground was vibrating. My hand shook as I struck the match. I

sensed it would be a bad
night. Already there were
distant explosions. Eric
squidged between our feet
and lay growling softly. I
think he was scared, too.

I hoped Dad was right about
lightning never striking twice in the same place.

'Where's Pearl?' Mrs Little asked anxiously.

'At Mrs Wilson's.'

'She shouldn't take that baby out at night,'
said Mrs Little. 'It's turning cold, and she won't
want to be stuck in a strange shelter . . .'

Rose went rigid. Her face was white and,
though her lips were moving, no sound was coming out.

'Rose?' I said. She was frightening me.
'Rose?'

Suddenly I knew what was wrong. 'Rose!' I
shrieked. 'Is the baby in the house?'

I'd thought Mum had taken him with her,

and all the time my stupid sister was supposed to be looking after him. I flung the door open and leapt up and out of the shelter.

'Fred!' Rose shouted. 'Be careful!'

Heavy planes droned above me, and lines of fire streaked up through the sky as our anti-aircraft guns shot at them. Bombs were exploding, thankfully not close, but I was scared – so scared. I burst in through Mrs Little's door, fell over goodness knows what and struggled through to the hall. As I leapt up the stairs, I heard the baby crying. I know he couldn't understand what was happening, but he sounded frightened to me.

I burst into Mum and Dad's room, scooped up the baby, his blankets and the bag Mum keeps beside the cot, marked 'Air raid'. It had nappies and stuff in it.

I hurtled downstairs, ducking every time I heard the thud of a bomb. Glass shattered nearby, and someone screamed.

Rather than risk tripping over Mrs Little's clutter with the baby in my arms, I went out the front and turned down the side alley towards the garden. Then, even over the sound of German engines, I heard a terrifying whistling sound, then there was an almighty, deafening, brain-banging crash.

The night was filled with dust and smoke. I

couldn't see. Eric was howling, but something must have happened to my ears, because it sounded so far away. I pulled the baby's blanket over his head, so he wouldn't choke, and stumbled down the garden. Where was the shelter?

My feet rocked over bricks as I lurched along, terrified I might fall and injure the baby. I couldn't see a thing, and I could barely breathe. Then the ground levelled out and I staggered onwards.

I sobbed with relief when I saw the hump of the shelter off to one side. 'Let me in!' I cried as I dived for the door. But the door wasn't there! I gripped the baby with one arm and pulled at what felt like a great chunk of wood with the other. It gave way and I bent and dived inside.

Sheer instinct must have helped me protect the baby, because I landed on my side. When I opened my eyes, there was no Rose, no Mrs Little.

I was looking into the snuffly snout of George. My pig.

That's where they found us.

I'd bumbled across one of the gaps where next door's wall had been smashed down. My poor mother was beside herself with terror for our safety and Rose couldn't stop sobbing.

All the windows at the front of our flat had been blown in by a bomb blast. There was glass everywhere. I nearly cried when I saw glass in the baby's cot. A framed photo of us all lay on the floor. When I picked it up, it fell apart. There was a folded piece of paper hidden in the back – Mum's always doing that, putting information and little messages inside frames. She says they'll make people happy when they find them in years to come. This one had a list of when and where we were born. I put it in my pocket. She'll have to add the baby's name – when he gets one.

We huddled together on cushions and blankets in Rose's bedroom. She made Mum have the bed with the baby. When they'd dropped off to sleep, for some reason I thought back to when I had measles, and everyone said I was jumping on the bed when I wasn't. I'd felt funny then, and I felt funny now. Nothing in particular – I just didn't feel, well, *normal*.

When Dad came home and got over the shock of seeing the house damaged and the thrill of finding us all right, there were explanations to be made. Mum and Dad were kind to Rose, and told her these things happen, and in the heat of the moment we all make mistakes. She drank a glass of nerve tonic, and was all right after a while.

Every so often, though, tears leaked out.

I explained about the pig, and Dad said we'll find a way of keeping it in our garden. Then we took Eric for a walk, and Dad told me how proud he is of me. 'You've worked hard at salvaging,' he said, 'but if you do nothing else in this war, Fred, you can honestly hold your head up and say, "I've done my bit."'

That made me feel good.

Dad said if it wasn't for me, the baby might easily have been killed by flying glass. He grinned. 'Time we gave Number Two Son a name.'

They've been tossing around ideas ever since he was born, but can't decide on anything. I'd like to have called him Biggles, but they weren't having that.

I gave up and went to bed. I felt peculiar. Not ill, or anything, just – weird. I told Mum and she said, 'You're not yourself at all, are you?'

Next morning, she brought me breakfast in

bed. Dad came in, too. I was just sinking my teeth into a slice of toast and dripping, when he said, 'We've decided on a name for Number Two Son.'

'What?' I said, expecting something wet, like Cyril.

Mum smiled. 'We're going to call him George.'

Oh no.

After breakfast, I got my jacket on ready for salvaging. The baby was outside in his pram, all happy, like there wasn't a war on.

I tickled his nose. 'I can't call you George,' I said. 'George is a pig's name. I think I'll call you Gee, for short – baby Gee.'

Toby opened his eyes and stared up at the ceiling. His own ceiling. His mouth felt greasy. 'Ugh! Dripping!' he muttered.

His chest suddenly thumped – as if a hammer had hit it.

'Gee!'

Toby rolled off the bed and slid on his knees towards the chest. He burrowed inside for the photograph. 'Gee. It's you. You were Fred's little brother.'

His brain felt like a snowstorm, whirling and spinning. Gee was born less than seventy years ago. Could he still be alive?

Feet thudded up the stairs. Jake. 'We've got to go down and Evie said hurry up, 'cos the ice is melting.' He stopped. 'You OK, Toby? What's up?'

Toby tried to swallow the lump in his throat.

'You go down,' he said. 'Tell Evie I'll be there in a minute. I've got . . . something to do.'

Jake, looking concerned, backed out of the door. 'OK. If you're sure.'

Toby turned back to the photo. 'Isn't there anything more you can tell me?' he asked the gentle face. Turning the frame over, he read the note once more, then stopped.

'I wonder . . .'

Had baby Gee grown up to copy his mother's habit of hiding things in frames? Toby got a pair of scissors and carefully, carefully slit the brown paper backing.

He nearly passed out when he saw a newspaper cutting and a folded sheet of paper inside. He glanced at the cutting. The headline said, 'House fire tragedy strikes local family. Two saved.' Without reading further, Toby folded the cutting. Then, taking a deep breath, he opened out the sheet of paper. It was a letter.

Dear Toby,

I'm going to hide this in my photo frame so it'll never get lost. One day, I know, curiosity will get the better of you, and you'll find it.

I fell out with my family when I was nineteen. I ran away and ended up in New Zealand where I started a family of my own. Tragedy struck – one dreadful day, which I can't bear to recall, you and I lost everything and everyone we had. Except each other.

Toby, I'm not well. I can't look after you. I will leave you somewhere safe. When I get better – if I get better – I will come for you.

I think, by the time you read this, you will have discovered our secret. Every so often, someone in our family is born with a special gift – the ability to learn about their past. In the hope that you inherit this gift, I leave you this wooden chest. It will be difficult for you, because you discovered the chest once before, and you can see the result! Piece names together, Toby, and go and find out who you are.

I hope you have a new family now. If you do, treasure them. Don't ever fall out with them. Accept their love. And always remember, I will love you till the day I die, for you are all I have.

Your loving grandfather Gee.

Toby sat back on his heels and cried.

✈ ✈ ✈

'Toby, love?'

It was Evie. Don was behind her, concerned.

'I've asked Jake to go, so we can be alone,' Evie said. 'Do you want to talk?'

'Oh, Evie, Don – I have got some family of my own – but I don't know where.'

'How do you know?' asked Don, and Toby thrust the newspaper cutting and letter into his hands.

His foster parents read silently, then, as one, turned to look at the names on the pinboard.

Toby nodded. 'I'll try and explain.'

'Not just now,' said Evie. 'Let's go for a walk, and we'll talk about how to start looking for your family. You need to know where you come from, Toby Tucker!'

Don grinned. 'Then we must think about more decorating.'

'More?' said Toby. 'I thought my room was the last.'

'Don means redecorating,' said Evie. 'The small bedroom's going to be a nursery for your little brother or sister.'

Toby felt a warm glow steal over him. I have got some family of my own, he thought, and some day I'll find them. But for now . . . He looked up at Evie and Don with shining eyes.

I already have a family.

EGMONT PRESS: ETHICAL PUBLISHING

Egmont Press is about turning writers into successful authors and children into passionate readers – producing books that enrich and entertain. As a responsible children's publisher, we go even further, considering the world in which our consumers are growing up.

Safety First
Naturally, all of our books meet legal safety requirements. But we go further than this; every book with play value is tested to the highest standards – if it fails, it's back to the drawing-board.

Made Fairly
We are working to ensure that the workers involved in our supply chain – the people that make our books – are treated with fairness and respect.

Responsible Forestry
We are committed to ensuring all our papers come from environmentally and socially responsible forest sources.

For more information, please visit our website at
www.egmont.co.uk/ethicalpublishing